MW00760880

Some Sheep

By Mark Shulman

Illustrated by
Vincent Nguyen
& Joe Bartos

BARRON'S

Some sheep turn left

Some sheep turn right

Some sheep get turned around at night

Some sheep step on
Some sheep step off

Some sheep run late
and wheeze and cough

Some sheep move in

Some sheep move out

Some sheep get stuck
and have to shout

Some sheep go far

Some sheep go near

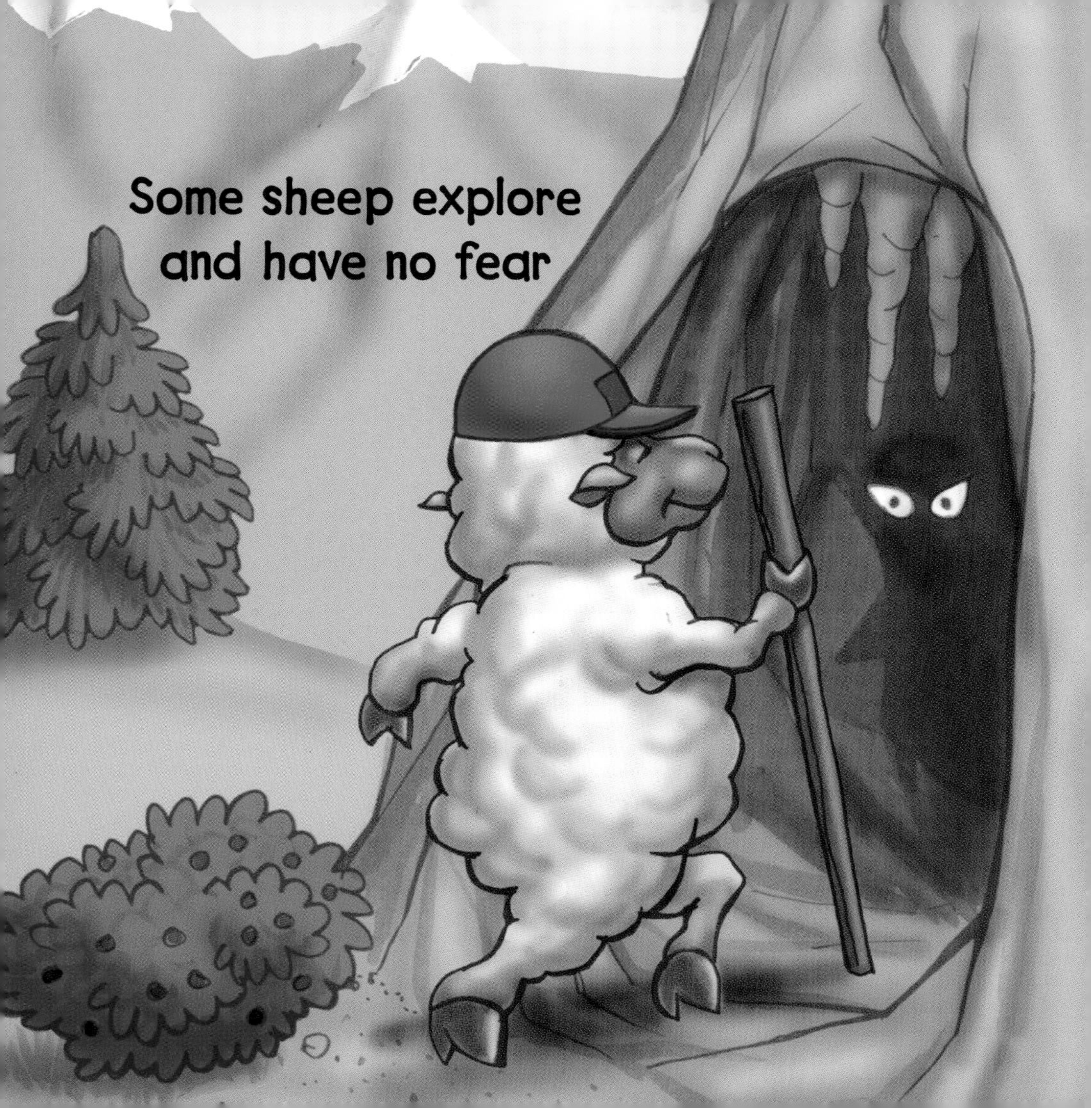
Some sheep explore
and have no fear

Some sheep throw high
Some sheep throw low

Some sheep are best
at tic-tac-toe

Some sheep in front
Some sheep behind

Some sheep get help
and they don't mind

Some sheep go through
Some sheep between

Some sheep will choose
the trampoline

Some sheep climb up

Some sheep climb down

Some sheep just swing
all over town

Some sheep go last
Some sheep go first

Some sheep have got
an awful thirst

Some sheep look here
Some sheep look there

Some sheep find
Mister Teddy Bear

Some sheep below
Some sheep above

And all sheep dream
of things they love

To Some Kids:

Hannah, Lily, Sophie, Isaac, Ethan, Emma, Chloe, Anders, Celia, Joseph, Victoria, DJ, Isabel, Sam, and Michael Chazanoff

First edition for North America published in 2003 by Barron's Educational Series, Inc.

Created at Oomf, Inc.
www.Oomf.com

By Mark Shulman
Illustrated by Vincent Nguyen and Joe Bartos
Designed by Joe Bartos

All inquiries should be addressed to:
Barron's Educational Series, Inc.
250 Wireless Boulevard
Hauppauge, New York 11788
http://www.barronseduc.com

International Standard Book No. 0-7641-5653-5
Library of Congress Catalog Card No. 2002113923
Printed in Singapore
9 8 7 6 5 4 3 2 1